HISTORICAL AGES

THE IRON AGE

BY HEATHER C. HUDAK

Core Library
An Imprint of Abdo Publishing
abdobooks.com

Cover image: Archaeologists have discovered Iron Age sites where blacksmiths once made tools out of iron.

abdobooks.com

Published by Abdo Publishing, a division of ABDO, PO Box 398166, Minneapolis, Minnesota 55439.

Printed in the United States of America, North Mankato, Minnesota.
102024
012025

Cover Photo: Science History Images/Alamy
Interior Photos: John Hopkins/Alamy, 4–5, 7; Red Line Editorial, 10; Smith Archive/Alamy, 12–13; Shutterstock Images, 15, 16, 26–27, 34–35, 43, 45; English Heritage/Heritage Images/Hulton Fine Art Collection/Getty Images, 20–21, 25, 32; M. Seemuller/DEA/De Agostini/Getty Images, 23 (top left); A. De Gregorio/DEA/De Agostini/Getty Images, 23 (top right); Album/Alamy, 23 (bottom left); Universal History Archive/Universal Images Group/Getty Images, 23 (bottom right), 36; TravelCollection/Image Professionals GmbH/Alamy, 29; Matthias Balk/dpa/picture alliance/Getty Images, 39

Editor: Laura Stickney
Series Designer: Ryan Gale

Library of Congress Control Number: 2024938361

Publisher's Cataloging-in-Publication Data

Names: Hudak, Heather C., author.
Title: The Iron Age / by Heather C. Hudak
Description: Minneapolis, Minnesota: ABDO Publishing, 2025 | Series: Historical ages | Includes online resources and index.
Identifiers: ISBN 9781098295646 (lib. bdg.) | ISBN 9798384916642 (ebook)
Subjects: LCSH: History, Ancient--Juvenile literature. | Iron age--Juvenile literature. | Clans and clan system--Juvenile literature. | Iron smelting--Juvenile literature. | Civilization and science--Juvenile literature. | History--Juvenile literature. | Historical archaeology--Juvenile literature. | Anthropology, Prehistoric--Juvenile literature.
Classification: DDC 930.16--dc23

CONTENTS

CHAPTER ONE

FARMING FOR ARTIFACTS

Third-generation farmer Gerry Fair never imagined that his land might hold clues to England's ancient past. In the 1960s, Fair took ownership of farmland in Poulton, England. He'd heard rumors that ancient Roman coffins had been discovered on the land in the 1940s. One day, Fair was looking at a map of his farm when he noticed something. There was a ruined chapel on the farm, along with sandstone blocks on the ground. Fair decided to start digging.

Archaeologists, volunteers, and students working with the Poulton Research Project have found artifacts from multiple historical periods at Gerry Fair's farm.

First, Fair dug up a piece of what he thought was an ancient floor tile. Fair tried to find someone to investigate the find, but no one seemed too excited about it. Later, in 1994, Fair discovered some old pottery after plowing the field near the chapel. He wondered if something important was hidden beneath the earth. He made some phone calls, and finally, a local archaeologist and a professor agreed to look at the site.

At first, Fair thought the experts weren't interested in what he had to show them. But that changed when the group uncovered human bones and ancient Roman pottery. Excavations began at Fair's farm in 1995 and continued for years after. Until these discoveries, there was little evidence of ancient settlements in northwest England.

Since then, archaeologists at Fair's farm have uncovered artifacts spanning about 11,000 years of history. They have found more than 5,000 artifacts dating to around 800 BCE. This period is known as the Iron Age. Some of the most noteworthy finds at

Archaeologists at the Poulton site have uncovered artifacts such as Iron Age coins, brooches, and dog remains. Fragments of human skeletons have also been found.

the farm include remains of homes, metalwork, jewelry, carved antlers, and pottery. Each artifact is a clue about how ancient peoples lived and died. Experts believe there is still much more to be discovered at the farm.

DIGGING INTO THE PAST

Archaeologists categorize ancient human history in the Old World, which includes Europe, Africa, and Asia, into three periods. These are the Stone Age, Bronze

Age, and Iron Age. Archaeologists use these names because most items remaining from these periods are made of stone or metal. During the Bronze Age, people developed advanced metalworking techniques. They formed large empires and trade networks.

In about 1200 BCE, many Bronze Age empires began to collapse. Historians are unsure why. Some possibilities include natural disasters and foreign invasions. Over time, the copper and tin needed to make bronze became harder to get. People started using iron because it was easier to find. This

THE SEA PEOPLE

At the end of the Bronze Age, the eastern Mediterranean was thriving. It was home to bronze trade routes. The region included Syria, Cyprus, Egypt, Palestine, and Anatolia. But then, groups of people invaded. These groups were known as the Sea People. Their exact origins and identities are unknown. They likely came to the Mediterranean in search of resources and a better way of life. They struggled for control of the lands, and empires fell. The collapse of trade routes and relationships caused a bronze shortage. This is one possible explanation for the end of the Bronze Age.

marked the transition from the Bronze Age to the Iron Age.

The Iron Age began at different times in various locations. It took time for people to develop ways to smelt iron. Smelting is the process of heating ore past its melting point. In the Middle East and eastern Mediterranean, the Iron Age began in about 1200 BCE and ended in around 550 BCE. Western ironworking techniques arrived in China in around 1000 BCE. Iron did not become widely used in the United Kingdom until about 800 BCE,

SMELTING

After smelting metal, people can shape it into different objects. Copper was the first metal that people smelted. They did so in about 5000 BCE. Early people used furnaces to smelt iron. One type was the bowl furnace. To make this furnace, people dug a small hole in the ground. Then they placed a bed of hot charcoal inside the hole and added the iron ore. They used a bellows to blow air through a pipe into the hole. This created a draft. When the ore was red-hot, people removed it with a tool. Then they hammered it into shapes. They reheated the ore over a fire to keep it hot.

THE BOWL FURNACE

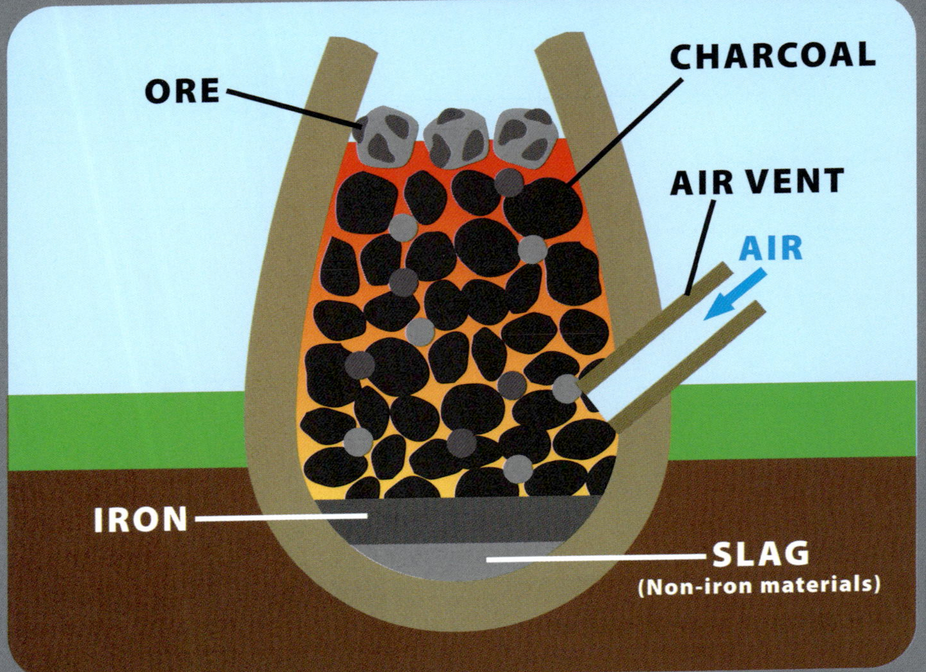

The bowl furnace was one of the earliest types of furnaces used for smelting. This diagram shows the different parts of the furnace. What do you notice about the parts of the furnace? Why do you think it was a useful tool for Iron Age people?

and the Iron Age ended there in 43 CE. Meanwhile, the Iron Age did not begin in Egypt until around 500 BCE.

The Iron Age was a time of discovery. New smelting technologies paved the way for advancements in the ways people lived. During this period, humanity took its first steps out of the ancient world and into the future.

STRAIGHT TO THE SOURCE

Archaeologist Kevin Cootes is a consultant for the Poulton Research Project, which oversees excavations at the Fair farm in Poulton, England. He spoke about the importance of the discoveries at Poulton:

> *Very little was known of high status Iron Age communities in the north west of England until now. We can tell from what we found that this community was very affluent, from trading along the river. Poulton is a well-preserved time capsule of thousands of years of life. It is not even a once in a lifetime find, it is a once in a thousand careers' find. It is absolutely fascinating and a privilege to be involved with.*

Source: Jacinta Bowler. "Archaeologists Uncover Exciting 'Time Capsule' of Iron Age Artifacts in England." *ScienceAlert*, 23 Feb. 2022, sciencealert.com. Accessed 17 Apr. 2024.

WHAT'S THE BIG IDEA?

Take a close look at this passage. What is the main point? What does the passage say about the importance of Iron Age excavations? What makes the findings at the Fair farm unique, and what clues do they provide about the past?

CHAPTER TWO

EARLY IRON USE

The earliest iron artifacts date to about 3000 BCE. But the iron used for these items probably came from meteorites, not iron ore. Meteoroids are rocklike objects from outer space. When they enter Earth's atmosphere, they cause a streak of light called a meteor. Once they hit the ground, they are called meteorites.

Meteoric iron did not require smelting, so it was easier for ancient people to work with. One of the earliest-known Egyptian artifacts

Two daggers, one made of gold and one made of meteoric iron, were discovered in King Tutankhamun's tomb. The iron dagger, *left*, measures about 13.4 inches (34 cm) long.

METEORIC IRON

Many meteorites contain metals such as iron. Some of the earliest descriptions of meteors are found in ancient Hittite writings. They are described as "fire from heaven." These texts support the belief that the Hittites were one of the first cultures to use iron from meteorites. Meteoric iron contains a metal called nickel. The nickel made the metal malleable, which meant it could be hammered into shape. This made meteoric iron easier to work with than iron ore, which required smelting. Smelting was not needed to produce early ironwork from meteoric iron.

made from meteoric iron is a dagger from King Tutankhamun's tomb. He was an Egyptian pharaoh who ruled from about 1333 BCE to 1324 BCE.

Between around 2000 BCE and 1500 BCE, people realized they could extract metal from iron ore. Iron smelting required a furnace that could reach temperatures high enough to make iron workable. The first people to work with iron ore were from Anatolia, which is now the Asian portion of Turkey, and Persia. Persia was in what is now the country of Iran.

Alaca Höyük is located near Corum, Turkey. The site features 13 tombs in which royal people were buried with bronze, iron, and gold artifacts.

People in these regions produced copper and bronze. They might have accidentally produced iron inside their copper-melting furnaces.

Iron was rare and highly valued during this time. Letters written by Assyrian traders in the 2000s BCE mention that iron was worth 40 times more than silver and 400 times more than tin. One of the oldest iron artifacts is a dagger with an iron blade and bronze handle. Archaeologists found it in a royal tomb at Alaca

The Hittites used bronze to make ceremonial objects called standards or sun disks. One bronze standard found at Alaca Höyük features bull and deer figures.

Höyük, an ancient settlement made by the Hattians in northern Anatolia. The settlement dates to 2500 BCE. The Hattians were the area's earliest-known inhabitants. Later, the Hittites invaded the region. Archaeologists have also found early iron artifacts at Kaman-Kalehöyük in Turkey. These include iron beads, knives, and axe heads dating to between 2200 BCE and 2000 BCE.

IRON AGE BEGINNINGS

The Iron Age did not begin when iron was first discovered. It took about 1,000 years for iron-smelting technology to become widely available. In around

1200 BCE, the Iron Age began with the regular use of iron across Anatolia and the Near East, located near the present-day Middle East. This region had rich iron deposits. Archaeologists debate who first discovered iron smelting. Many believe Hittites were the first. Archaeologists have found ancient texts that describe how Hittites traded iron objects with Assyrians and Egyptians.

Although the Hittites had long

KAMAN-KALEHÖYÜK

Kaman-Kalehöyük was located in an area of central Anatolia ruled by the Hittites. The Hittites first appeared in Anatolia in about 2000 BCE. They formed a massive empire and were known for producing bronze. Kaman-Kalehöyük was one of the main Iron Age mound sites on Hittite lands. It was located along trade routes. It might have been a hub for trading goods with people from different regions. Today, Kaman-Kalehöyük is an archaeological site. Archaeologists have found copper, bronze, and iron artifacts there. The artifacts date from the Middle Bronze Age in about 1950 BCE to the Iron Age in about 600 BCE.

used furnaces to smelt copper and tin for bronze, they had to develop new furnaces to smelt iron. These furnaces produced iron blooms, or rough, spongy balls of iron. Blooms contained slag, or non-iron materials. Blacksmiths hammered the blooms to remove the slag. They used charcoal furnaces to heat the blooms before hammering them into shape. Carbon from the charcoal combined with the iron to form a type of steel, which was harder than bronze or copper. Iron was more difficult to work with than other metals. But it became popular because of its strength and availability.

The Hittite empire collapsed around 1200 BCE, near the beginning of the Iron Age. Archaeologists are unsure why. The Assyrians took over many areas that were once ruled by the Hittites. The Assyrians were from Mesopotamia, located in Iraq and parts of Iran, Kuwait, Syria, and Turkey. They ruled parts of the Middle East from about 1400 BCE to 600 BCE. The Assyrians used Hittite iron-smelting methods to become major iron producers.

STRAIGHT TO THE SOURCE

Evidence of early ironwork is rare. But ancient letters suggest that Hittites traded for iron wares. The following is from a letter written by the Hittite king to the Assyrian king in the 1200s BCE:

> *Concerning the good iron which you mentioned in your letter, the store in Kizzuwatna has run out of good iron. I wrote to you that it is not a suitable time to produce iron. They will produce iron but they have not finished yet. When they have finished I will send it to you. Now I am sending you an iron (sword/dagger) point.*

Source: Nathaniel L. Erb-Satullo. "The Innovation and Adoption of Iron in the Ancient Near East." *Journal of Archaeological Research*, 21 Feb. 2019, link.springer.com. Accessed 17 Apr. 2024.

CONSIDER YOUR AUDIENCE

Adapt this passage for a different audience, such as your friends. Write a blog post conveying this same information for the new audience. How does your post differ from the original text and why?

CHAPTER THREE

IRON AGE IMPACT

Though the discovery of iron smelting did not happen at the same time in all parts of the world, it had a significant impact on many societies. When the Iron Age started, most people were farmers. They made their own tools and clothes, built their own homes, and grew food. Early Iron Age people likely lived in villages of about 50 to 80 people. They came together to handle big tasks, such as tending fields. Iron tools made their jobs easier. They used iron to

Early Iron Age people used farming tools such as sickles and plows. At Old Oswestry Hillfort in England, Iron Age farmers raised animals such as cattle.

CLUES TO THE PAST

In the 1990s, archaeologists found the remains of the oldest-known iron-smelting furnaces at Tell Hammeh in what is now northern Jordan. The furnaces dated to about 930 BCE, although some experts think ironwork in the area might have started earlier than that. At that time, modern-day Jordan was part of the Levant, a region along the eastern Mediterranean coast. It included present-day Israel, Lebanon, and Syria. Tell Hammeh is located near several iron ore deposits.

make farming tools, such as sickles. These are cutting tools with curved blades. People also used iron to make rotary querns, or tools for grinding grain.

Iron tools helped farmers dig into tough soils and harvest crops efficiently. Soon, they began expanding their fields. Bigger fields meant farmers could produce more crops. Because more food was available, people had larger families and longer lifespans.

People also had more time for other activities such as blacksmithing and woodworking. They sold or traded goods they produced. Some people offered

IRON AGE VS. BRONZE AGE TOOLS

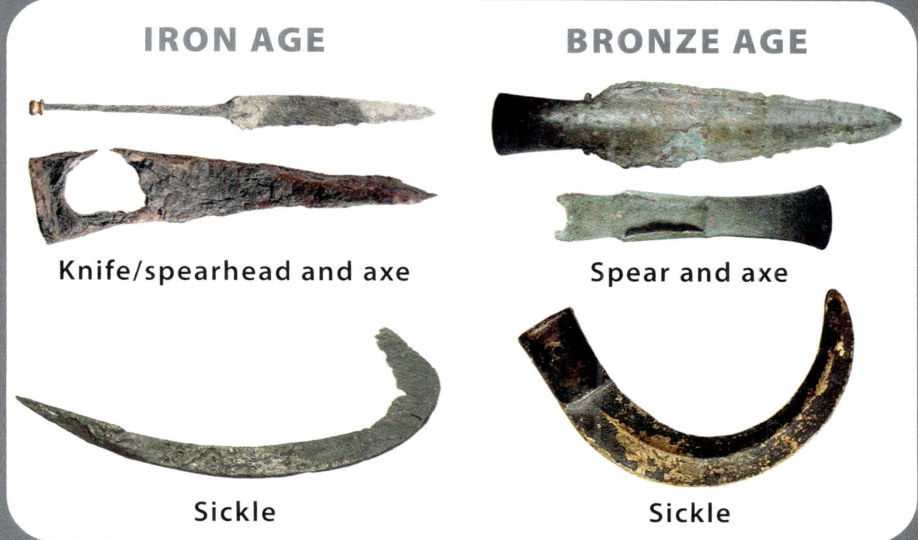

During the Iron Age, people used iron to make many different types of tools. This chart shows examples of common Iron Age tools and common Bronze Age tools. What do you notice about these tools? How are they similar and different?

services to others, and jobs other than farming began to take shape. Meanwhile, more permanent settlements formed. Cities, towns, and empires grew.

FORMING BOUNDARIES

As communities formed, people drew territorial lines. This meant conflicts between communities became more common. People used iron to create weapons. Because iron was easy to find, a large army could be quickly equipped with iron swords. This was not possible with bronze. The development of iron weapons led to more warfare. Carburized-iron swords were sharper and stronger than bronze ones. They could also do more damage than bronze weapons, which were brittle. Carburization is a heating process that hardens iron. As the metal is heated, it absorbs carbon. This element is found in natural objects such as plants and animals. The Assyrians were the first to make iron weapons and armor, which gave them an advantage in battle.

CARBURIZATION

Carburizing is a heat treatment that turns a low-carbon metal into a high-carbon metal. This is done by exposing the metal to a large amount of carbon. The carbon attaches to the outside of the metal, giving it a hard shell. This makes the metal stronger and more durable. The higher the heat and the longer the metal is exposed to the carbon, the stronger the metal will be.

Iron Age hillforts included sloping barriers of earth, wood, and stone. There are more than 4,000 Iron Age hillforts throughout England and Ireland.

The increase in warfare meant communities needed to protect themselves from attackers. Some people built hillforts on high ground, putting up walls for protection. They dug ditches around their settlements.

FURTHER EVIDENCE

Chapter Three includes information about life during the Iron Age. What is the main point of this chapter? What key evidence supports this point? Go to the article about Iron Age societies at the website below. Find a quote from the website that supports the chapter's main point.

WHAT WAS LIFE LIKE IN THE IRON AGE?

abdocorelibrary.com/iron-age

CHAPTER FOUR

IRON AGE IN EUROPE

In ancient times, countries in Eurasia were closely connected by conflicts and trade routes. Over time, eastern Mediterranean traders and warriors brought ironworking to other parts of the continent. It spread from the Middle East to India and the central and eastern Mediterranean.

In around 1200 BCE, iron became more common in everyday life. By about 1050 BCE, the Iron Age was at its height in Greece, Cyprus, Macedonia, and Crete.

Archaeologists have discovered Iron Age artifacts in the ancient city of Kourion in Cyprus. Today, people can visit the ruins of the city.

Archaeologists have found iron knives and daggers from the 1200s BCE in Kition and Kourion, ancient cities in Cyprus. These findings suggest that iron was not only used for special occasions. It was part of daily life.

At Teppe Hasanlu in Iran, archaeologists found about 2,000 iron artifacts dating from around 1100 BCE to 800 BCE. These include arrowheads, swords, sickle blades, and pins. Teppe Hasanlu was an iron production center during the early Iron Age. It was located along trade routes between Anatolia and Mesopotamia. At the site, archaeologists also found graves. One grave had iron and ironworking tools inside it, suggesting that the person buried there might have been a metalworker. The grave was found near the graves of warriors, who usually had a higher status in society. This might mean metalworkers had a higher status too.

The widespread use of iron in India happened in around 1200 BCE. In the Ganges Valley in northern India, archaeologists found iron tools dating to around 1400 BCE. People likely used these tools to clear land

Archaeologists have uncovered city walls and a cemetery at Teppe Hasanlu. Numerous pieces of art have also been found at the site, including a golden bowl.

for rice paddies. These are small fields that are flooded with water and used to grow rice.

HALLSTATT CULTURE

In around 1100 BCE, iron use spread across central and western Europe. One significant central European Iron Age site is by Lake Hallstatt in Austria. Artifacts from the Hallstatt Culture were found at the site in 1846 CE.

The Hallstatt Culture existed between 800 BCE and 450 BCE. It was made up of groups in southern Germany, Switzerland, eastern France, eastern Austria, Bohemia, and the Balkans. These groups were connected by a vast trade network. They had similar tools, housing, utensils, and farming methods.

During the Bronze Age and Iron Age, the area in and around Hallstatt was known for its rich iron and salt deposits. These salt deposits led to a salt trade. In about 500 BCE, salt and other resources in the area began running out. The Hallstatt Culture declined. Other groups developed, including the La Tène Culture. This culture gets its name from a site in northern Switzerland called La Tène. The La Tène Culture dominated the area from about 450 BCE to 50 BCE.

CELTIC CULTURE

The civilization of ancient Greece flourished in around 1000 BCE. It included present-day Greece, parts of Turkey's western coast, and cities in the Mediterranean and along the Black Sea. Ancient Rome was founded in 753 BCE. It was centered around the city of Rome. The Romans were influenced by the culture, religion, and architecture of Greek colonies south of Rome.

Both ancient Greece and ancient Rome were powerful civilizations. They were known for innovations in politics, art, religion, and engineering.

Ancient Greeks and Romans referred to people who lived north of the Mediterranean as Celts. The Celtic culture included many groups. They were connected by the Celtic language and had similar ways of life. Celts lived in hierarchical societies with rulers and warriors at the top. Next in importance were religious leaders called druids, trades workers, and farmers. Celtic peoples lived throughout western

CELTIC BELIEFS

Druids were priests, teachers, and judges. They were high-ranking members of Celtic societies. They were well-respected and held power. Anyone who disobeyed a druid could face punishment. Druids often led religious ceremonies. They worshipped in natural places, such as groves and stone circles. Druids believed in spirits. They tossed valuable objects, such as weapons and metalwork, into bodies of water as an offering to spirits.

Some Iron Age people, such as the Celts, lived in roundhouses with thatched roofs. These homes had hearths in the center for lighting fires.

and central Europe, including in Ireland and the United Kingdom.

People from continental Europe brought ironworking to the British Isles in about 800 BCE. Archaeologists are unsure what Iron Age life was like in the area. However, Iron Age sites have been found across the region. Maiden Castle, the first Iron Age hillfort, was built in Dorset, England, in around 800 BCE. At its peak in 400 BCE to 200 BCE, it was one of the largest hillforts in Europe. Its earthwork ramparts reach up to 20 feet (6 m) high in some places.

In 55 BCE and 54 BCE, Roman emperor Julius Caesar raided settlements in the United Kingdom.

But the Romans eventually left the area. The Romans were powerful fighters with a big army. They expanded their territory across the Mediterranean and Europe before arriving in the United Kingdom.

Over the next 100 years, rulers in the United Kingdom maintained friendly relationships with Roman rulers. But in 43 CE, Roman emperor Claudius sent an army to invade the United Kingdom. This event marked the beginning of the end of the Iron Age in the United Kingdom.

WRITING SYSTEMS

During the Iron Age, people across Europe, Africa, and parts of Asia began developing more complex writing systems. In about 1300 BCE, the Phoenicians developed a writing system with 22 characters. Phoenicia was a region along the Mediterranean coast near Lebanon. It included parts of present-day Syria and Israel. Each character in the Phoenician alphabet represented a sound. Before the Phoenician alphabet, many early writing systems used symbols. Greeks and Romans used the Phoenician alphabet as a basis for their writing systems.

CHAPTER FIVE

IRON AGE IN CHINA AND EGYPT

Archaeologists do not know exactly when iron-smelting technology was first discovered in China. There is little evidence of such technology in China. Some archaeologists think early people in China gained knowledge of iron smelting between 1600 BCE and 1100 BCE. They likely learned about Western ironworking techniques in around 1000 BCE. However, early people in China had already developed their own smelting technologies. They also developed

A sculpture at the Kailuan Museum in Tangshan, Hebei Province, China, shows what smelting might have looked like during China's Han dynasty.

Archaeologists have found many different objects from China's Iron Age, including mirrors made of silver, iron, and bronze.

kilns for pottery firing. A combination of these innovations led to the discovery of new ironworking techniques in around 800 BCE.

Iron-smelting furnaces in China could reach temperatures hot enough to liquefy iron. People could then pour the iron into molds to make different shapes, such as pots, plows, and artwork. This was known as cast iron. People in China were the first to use it. Cast-iron farm tools were stronger and more durable than tools made from other materials. This made the tools more effective at working the soil. Cast-iron tools were also faster to make. It took less time to pour iron into molds than to forge it into shapes by hand. This meant iron tools could be made more efficiently, and more people had access to them. Farmers could afford better tools, which led to better food production. Higher food production caused the population to grow.

The earliest-known cast-iron objects in China were found in a cemetery in Shanxi province and a tomb in Jiangsu province. They date back to about 700 BCE to 800 BCE. They were made from white cast iron, which was too brittle to use for mass production. However, by about 600 BCE, people in China had discovered ways to make cast iron stronger. Archaeologists have found hoes and adzes in Henan province that

ANNEALING

Cast iron has a lot of carbon in it. This makes it easy to crack. Around 600 BCE, people in China found a way to reduce the amount of carbon. This process is called annealing. The cast iron is reheated slowly until it turns red-hot. It is then cooled to room temperature. Annealing makes it easier to bend and shape iron without breaking it.

have white cast iron in the center. The tools have an outer layer of carburized steel.

The people of China carefully guarded their knowledge of cast iron. It gave them an advantage, and they did not want other countries to learn about it. Western regions did not discover how to make cast iron until about 1400 CE.

IRON IN EGYPT

The Egyptians were some of the earliest people to make objects from iron. As of 2024, the earliest-known iron objects are meteoric-iron beads found in Egypt. They date to about 3300 BCE. But nearly 3,000 years passed before the Egyptians began to use iron in large amounts. The Iron Age in Egypt began in around 500 BCE.

Archaeologists don't know why it took so long for iron to become commonplace across Egypt. Some think

Archaeologists continue to uncover Iron Age artifacts and learn more about the period. In 2023, an Iron Age Celtic settlement was discovered in Munich, Germany.

it might have taken longer for smelting knowledge to reach Egypt because the region was located farther from Anatolia. Others believe there was a lack of iron ore and a lack of wood and coal to fuel furnaces.

MODERN-DAY IRON AGE

Some archaeologists debate whether the Iron Age ever ended and if it continues to this day. No new material was developed that replaced iron in the way that bronze replaced stone and iron replaced bronze. Iron is still essential to modern society. Iron in the form of steel is used for buildings, vehicles, and more. Steel is an alloy, or a metal made by mixing two other metals together. It is made by mixing iron and carbon. Although new technologies have been developed, the basic processes used to make iron and steel haven't changed much since the Iron Age.

ESSENTIAL ELEMENT

The Iron Age lasted until about 500 BCE. However, the period ended later in some parts of the world, such as Egypt, China, and the United Kingdom. It was a time of discovery and change.

Iron-smelting knowledge created new opportunities for communities around the world. Stronger, more durable iron tools made daily tasks, such as farming, much easier. Populations boomed, settlements formed, and new jobs were born. The use of iron to mass-produce weapons led to bigger armies and more brutal conflicts than before. Over time, people continued to refine iron techniques to help advance society. Thousands of years later, iron has remained essential in all parts of the world.

EXPLORE ONLINE

Chapter Five talks about the Iron Age in different regions. The article at the website below goes into more depth on this topic. Does the article answer any of the questions you had about the Iron Age?

IRON AGE

abdocorelibrary.com/iron-age

IMPORTANT DATES

3000 BCE
People make the earliest-known iron artifacts from meteoric iron.

2000–1500 BCE
Early people realize they can extract metal from iron ore.

1200 BCE
Bronze Age empires begin to collapse. The Iron Age begins in the Middle East and eastern Mediterranean. The widespread use of iron begins in India.

1100 BCE
Iron use spreads across the central and western parts of Europe.

1000 BCE
Knowledge of Western ironworking techniques arrives in China.

800–450 BCE

Iron becomes widely used in the United Kingdom. While the Iron Age ends between 550 BCE and 500 BCE in most parts of the world, it begins in Egypt in 500 BCE.

450–50 BCE

The La Tène Culture replaces the Hallstatt Culture as the dominant culture in central and western Europe.

1994–1995 CE

Gerry Fair discovers Iron Age artifacts on his farm in England. Archaeological excavations begin at the site.

STOP AND THINK

Dig Deeper

After reading this book, what questions do you still have about the Iron Age? With an adult's help, find a few reliable sources that can help you answer your questions. Write a paragraph about what you learned.

Say What?

Studying periods in ancient history can mean learning a lot of new vocabulary. Find five words in this book you've never heard before. Use a dictionary to find out what they mean. Then write the meanings in your own words and use each word in a new sentence.

Another View

This book talks about cast-iron technology in ancient China. As you know, every source is different. Ask a librarian or another adult to help you find a second source about this topic. Write a short essay comparing and contrasting the new source's point of view with that of this book's author. What is the point of view of each author?

Take a Stand

Some archaeologists wonder whether the Iron Age truly ended because no new material replaced iron. Archaeologists debate if the Iron Age actually continues to this day. Do you agree that the Iron Age continues today? Or do you think it really ended? Explain your answer.

GLOSSARY

archaeologist
a person who studies human history through artifacts and other remains

bellows
devices used to blow air onto a fire; made up of two handles that are used to squeeze an air bag

brittle
describing a material that is hard but breaks easily

empire
a political unit made up of territories or groups of people

excavations
acts of digging up the ground to uncover artifacts or remains

extract
to remove or take out

hierarchical
organized according to rank, status, or importance

ore
a solid natural material from which one or more minerals or metals can be extracted

territorial
of or relating to the ownership of a certain area

ONLINE RESOURCES

To learn more about the Iron Age, visit our free resource websites below.

Visit **abdocorelibrary.com** or scan this QR code for free Common Core resources for teachers and students, including vetted activities, multimedia, and booklinks, for deeper subject comprehension.

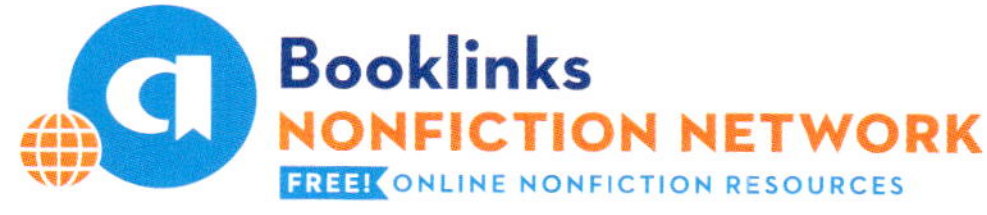

Visit **abdobooklinks.com** or scan this QR code for free additional online weblinks for further learning. These links are routinely monitored and updated to provide the most current information available.

LEARN MORE

Howell, Izzi. *The Genius of the Stone, Bronze, and Iron Ages*. Crabtree, 2020.

Kaiser, Emma. *The Bronze Age*. Abdo, 2025.

INDEX

About the Author

Heather C. Hudak has written hundreds of books for kids about all kinds of topics. When she's not writing, Heather enjoys traveling the world. She has been to about 60 countries, including Indonesia, Uruguay, Norway, and many other places in between. She has visited countless ancient sites, including the Acropolis in Greece, Angkor Wat in Cambodia, and Kohunlich in Mexico.